Short Stories

AUTHOR: KHALIL ISAAC MATHAI

COMPILED BY: JISHNU J

EDITING AND COVER DESIGN: JIBIN JAMES

Index

The House of Cats

There were seven cats in the house. There was a black cat and a white cat and half dozen spotted and patchy ones. The astute reader would now pause to reflect that this is bad arithmetic. One plus one plus half a dozen would make eight, not seven. This however, is the substance of the story. Most rules of science and mathematics we know today, do not apply to cats. Maybe, as we evolve in our understanding we will, one day master catemathics. But we are digressing. Let's us get back to our story. Regarding the debate on exactitude of the number of cats, we will just accede that the house was run over and run, by cats.

I remember fondly, a time, when I was a toddler. I used to be the focus of all attention. If there was a valuable trinket in the house, to be broken- I did it. If there were biscuit crumbs all over the Persian carpet, or a spilt bowl of ice cream, the yell went out for me – not for blacky or spotty. I guess it was too good to last.

Life changed when we took a kitten into our house. One day, an underfed kitten 'strayed' into our courtyard and was found mewing outside my parents' bedroom window. This was probably the oldest trick in the book, but my dad fell for it- hook, line, and whiskers.

We took the kitten into our house and named her- 'Whiskers'. Whiskers was easy to love and easier to train. There were a few discomfiting remarks by my dad, comparing my extended diaper phase in infancy to that of whiskers. Unfavourable comparisons apart, even I, a confirmed cat critic admired Whiskers meticulous exactitude and immaculate cleanliness. Her obsession for cleanliness would have prompted psychiatric intervention and electric shock treatment in a human. But she was a cat and for cats, as we discussed earlier, rules do not apply. Obsessive compulsive disorder diagnoses are hence confined to humans.

A red cushion on a teak-wood stool was established as her throne. It was from here, that she reigned, descending occasionally to dine from an elegantly designed bowl of bone-china. She had dispatched a stainless-steel saucer which an errant maid had allotted to her, to the corner of the kitchen, with an elegant back foot kick which Pele in his prime would have been proud of. Whiskers prospered and there was peace and prosperity in her empire.

One day whiskers gave birth to three kittens. Maybe it was four but as I said earlier, with cats, rules and numbers do not make sense. This obstetric event caught the house by surprise. My parents would any day have stood surety for her saintly character. The black Tom cat, who was seen around, had been considered by the family to be an odd job's man, called in by Whiskers for mundane jobs like rat catching.

With four odd cats in a three human house, the controlling interest had been lost. The Whisker family now moved in to the front room, literally and figuratively. All activities in the house were under catly supervision, all occasions, presided over. Nothing was spoken – there were no threats. Whiskers were too suave and sophisticated for that. They discreetly checked out all guests, inspected all purchases and diligently monitored the kitchen. There was a futuristic flavour to our house, rather like in a robotic era; we humans were guests and the cats were in control. It was indeed remarkable, that this control was achieved without violence and without a fuss. The occasional raised eyebrow or an upturned Whisker sufficed.

Like all growing corporates, the Whiskers were keen on expanding their empire. For this, they required fresh recruitment. Two neighbourhood stray cats were co-opted. They knew their place- they were not family. They would wait patiently during meals; only after the Whiskers had dined – would they move in. The generosity and munificence of the whisker clan was becoming legendary in catly circles. We had other cat visitors too. Some stayed on, some just passed through- probably travelling sales-kittens.

The reign of the Whiskers would have gone on, unchallenged, if it were not for a new entrant in to the household.

 Tuttu was a Lhapso puppy. He was gifted to me on my tenth birth day by a cousin pursuing greener pastures in Australia. The normally unflapple Whiskers were taken by surprise. Quick messages were passed to the entire clan. The Whiskers lined up along the walls to inspect and annihilate the potential menace. The swish of savage

claws being unsheathed, claws which had been honed to a point at the expense of the beautiful Persian rug, alerted my dad. A pre-emptive strike by my dad dispersed the murderous mob for the moment. The battle lines had been drawn.

With a massed frontal assault being thwarted, ambushes and other terrorist tactics became the rule of the day. Most of these ambushes were planned and executed at times when my father was out of the house. Tuttu would be found whelping in a corner of the room- nursing some tender part of his anatomy, which had been subject to the wrong end of a set of sharpened claws. At these times, when we investigated, the Whiskers were either absent from the scene of carnage, or conducting mass, in the room, with saintly expressions on their faces.

Tuttu was obviously the looser of this low intensity conflict. His confidence and his tail drooped; there were patchy holes in his morale and in his fur coat. The ultimate outcome never seemed to be in doubt. But then, Ma Whiskers made a tactical blunder. The reason why, this astute queen of cat-dom made this obviously fatal move is debated even today by students. There are many who opine that the scene was orchestrated, as the family had already planned a shift for strategic reasons. I believe that the long period of unquestioned

reign had softened the sharpness of Ma Whisker's instincts.

One morning my dad had settled with the morning paper, smoke curling out of the clay pipe in his mouth when all hell broke loose in the living room. He rushed in to find a whelping mass of fur in acute danger of being eviscerated by a fat cat. A broom snatched from a horrified servant restored peace. Then dad reached for his cane. This cane had a sting like a serpent. I can vouch for it. The cane was administered with controlled abandon. For the first time in her life, Whiskers had been chastised.

There is an eerie silence after an intense conflict- any war journalist will attest to that. In this silence Lady Whiskers picked herself up, dusted her coat, silenced

onlookers with a steely glance and then stalked majestically out of the house. The rest of the Whiskers clan stayed back only to tie up a few loose ends before they packed and departed. There were a few unconfirmed rumours about immigration rules to Canada being temporarily relaxed. We have no other clue to the clan's whereabouts. The stragglers stayed back, scavengers around the kitchen. But the era of cats was at an end. The house was mine again. Tuttu or his kin would never usurp the young master's privileges. They were not cats after all.

****

The Fisherman

"The city of Mumbai once belonged to us" Ramdu was telling his friends as they set out for the nights fishing. "Look at it today". The amount of money, these rich children throw away in a night could feed our entire community for a month". The weather was playing up a bit. The monsoon showers were still a month away. The sea was turbulent in anticipation. The catch had been poor for the past one week. Once the rain hit, they would be living off their savings for a month.

Every night, when the rest of the city headed home for a well-earned rest or the young punks headed out to town to squander their parents ill earned fortunes, work began for Ramdu and his friends. The bevy of boats from the village, polished and painted to protect the wood work would head out for the nights fishing.

There were many ships at anchorage. Ramdu and his friends could hear the familiar sounds as their boats chugged past. Most of the ships were cargo carriers, waiting for their turn to disgorge their contents. Two large oil tankers waited for their turn to berth. To their left Ramdu could see the flames of Uran where excess gas from the facility was burned off. To their right the nights and sounds of Bombay city slowly receded into the mist. The Taj Hotel was lit up in all its glory. Ramdu had a friend who worked as a cleaner in one of the hotel kitchens. The amount of unconsumed food the hotel dumped every night could have fed have the local slum population. The management however demurred. There would be too many issues. Political parties

could rake up issues of ethnic pride. If ever, there was a case of food poisoning in the slum, the hotel could be blamed and possibly gutted. So they dissociated themselves. The fishes in the bay were not choosy and did not vote. They enjoyed the food that the hotel could not use. The slum dwellers starved. Local organizations sensationalized the changes in the ecological system this food disposal was causing. They were bought off with honorary memberships to the hotels' discotheque. Ramdu fantasized about winning a lottery and then spending a couple of days in the hotel. It was not worth it, he decided. There was nothing the hotel offered which he did not have. The food was better at home and the liquor was as strong.

They were now passing the light house at the harbor entrance. Built by the British, the precision and resilience of this and the

Prongs light house fascinated Ramdu. The system still worked with kerosene lamps and giant prisms. As a child, his uncle Michael had once taken the boys to the light house for a picnic. The light house master had been gifted a box of prawns. In gratitude, the man had shown the boys around the array of giant prisms barely chipped despite years of wear. Ramdu contrasted this to the later constructions made by successive Indian governments. There was no government-built building which had survived a decade. The British, built monuments still stood proud.

The fishing boat was in the open sea now. Shoals of flying fish guided their path as they cruised with their fluttering fins on both sides of the boat before landing with a splash back in to the sea. A couple of dolphins followed their boat, confident with years of experience, that the fishermen would not harm them. Dolphins were a

fisherman's friend. They kept sharks at the bay. Ramdu remembered some of the nastier battles they had had with hungry sharks. The sharks would come, attempting to eat into their catch. It was only the sharp heavy hooks they carried, which could drive these marauders away. They just had to wound a shark and the rest of the predators would turn on their wounded friend, tearing him to bits. Just cut out for contemporary politics- thought Ramdu. Dolphins kept the sharks at bay. They were too smart for the sharks and would butt them in tender spots.

The boats had turned starboard. Pundits with their dopplers predicted a better catch off the Gujarat coast. They could see the Marine Drive with its endless streams of cars shimmering the Queens' necklace.

There were revelers on Chaupatty beach. A festival was on. The devout and the deviant jostled one another for a spot in the sand. A stage had been rigged. A local music band

belted out the latest Bollywood numbers. Hoardings and balloons lit up the sky. Boats conveying clients to the floating restaurant and the occasional speed boat still plied near the coast. There had been a grandiose project to link Nariman point to the main land by a bridge. Hundreds of politicians and administrators would become millionaires if the project ever materialized

- Ramdu mused.

He marveled at the government's Orwellian efficiency. He remembered the time when he had been late in paying his fishing tax. Within a week- his boat had been seized. His license was confiscated. It had taken him a month of visiting various Babu's offices, each with an official and an unwritten toll, before he could fish again. They never missed a trick. If they could trace a fishing boat which missed its taxes by a week, surely the big fish could be caught. Ramdu mused. The rot runs deep- he

surmised. The smalltime cop had to shake down the poor. The more powerful bled the rich. But ultimately everyone was happy. Ramdu shook his head. He had to focus on his fishing. He switched on his mini sonar- looking for fish shoals. Where were they hiding...?

A shout from the nearby boats snapped Ramdu to alertness. They were pointing towards the city. A flame of fire had enveloped the stage. The boom of the bomb now reached them. There had been a terrorist attack. Two fast boats could now be seen- from the beach- heading out to open sea. Ramdu looked behind. In the open sea there was a ship. A flashing light was guiding the escaping boats. Ramdu thought fast. It was obvious that the boats were making their getaway. Police sirens and pandemonium reigned. Fires silhouetted the night sky as shops and stalls caught fire. Hundreds must have died. No one seemed to

have noticed the fleeing speed boats. No one could stop them- unless!!

"Put out the lights and spread your nets"- Ramdu ordered. The fisher men knew the stakes involved. The men in the speed boats were desperate and possibly highly trained. If they discovered Ramdus plans, there could be hell to pay. The fishing boats quietly spread out- their nets all set to snag the big fish headed their way. The first speed boat was caught by surprise. There was a loud crack as a propeller broke. Two of the masked men within were flung into the water. They heard curses from the boat. A silenced automatic weapon opened up. Sheets of metal tore up Ramdus cabin and destroyed his radar. There was a shouted voice of command. The firing stopped. The second terrorist boat had reached the site now. The men climbed into it out of their, disabled boat. The second boat cruised around the fishing boats before heading for

their mother ship. The terrorists could be clearly seen now. Masked men, cradling automatic weapons- pointed at the fishing boats. Ramdu realized that the terrorists did not want to draw attention by any gunfire. The boat disappeared towards the ship and minutes later the schooner was on its way.

The fishermen inspected their nets. They were beyond repair. They freed the boat from the tangled ropes and after removing its motor- let it drift away. There could be no more fishing tonight and Ramdus boat required repairs. The fisherman refrained from informing the police. The terrorist ship

would have disappeared into international waters. Any
interaction with the Police would give the cops leverage to ply some money out of the fisher folk.

The damaged boat belonging to the terrorists was discovered washed up near the Haji Ali Mosque. A brilliant detective wrote up a story of a how a Police boat chased the fugitive vessel. The
terrorists had been shot- but the bodies could not be recovered. Two inspectors and a posse of policemen were decorated and promoted for the daredevil chase. Ramdu pawned his wife's bracelet for the first installment towards a new radar. The rains would let up soon. Fishing had to start again.

*****

Melinda

"There is something wrong with that dog".
My cousin commented. "She has been running around the block, barking and howling ever since I came here. I tried to feed her some bread and milk, but she ignored it and kept running". "Oh; that is Melinda. I will tell you the story of Melinda".

Melinda was a stray dog. I saw her for the first time a year ago, surrounded by a bevy of squealing pony tailed girls. The girls were trying to feed her and simultaneously garland her with a necklace of wild flowers. She seemed exceptionally well behaved for a stray and kept prancing playfully around the children with eager abandon. "What is her name? I asked Shilpa, the senior most of

the girls. "Melinda, said Shilpa, and so Melinda she was.

Melinda was one of the friendliest canines I have seen. She would greet each member of our colony, with vigorous wagging of her tail and whelps of joy. Even the few skeptics who had difficulty in conceding that affection was not always motivated by a desire for reward conceded that Melinda was different. Some of the socially correct and secretly ambitious women in the colony raised clichéd objections. Melinda could bite the children, the children vouched that she would not; she had fleas-so what? In the end everybody tolerated her. Some residents with secret hostility would douche her with buckets of water, if she slept on their porches. Melinda accepted these indignities with nonchalance.

Melinda was quite an athlete. An enterprising neighbour made a wicket gate to keep her out of the building. Melinda scoffed at this attempt at apartheid and would jump over this obstacle with alacrity. One day a servant maid in the colony noted that Melinda's tummy was looking a bit swollen. Melinda was expecting puppies. She seemed to be a desperate hurry to look for a safe place for brood. Melinda chose a corner of our neighbor's garden. The colony children were agog with excitement. Appropriate doggie names were being deliberated and debated.

Melinda gave birth to four puppies late one evening after the children had retired to their homes. Early next morning the colony was roused by the sound of frenzied barking. A distraught Melinda was charging up and down the block, howling. Someone had stolen her puppies. There were rumours that some colony residents had paid the alcoholic gardener to get rid of the brood. Melinda had been lured to a corner of the garden

 with a meal and the puppies abducted. "She will get over it", our neighbour said. Melinda never did get over her loss. Many months have gone by. She still runs madly around the block, desperately searching for the puppies she cannot find.

*****

Shehnaz

"A good house maid in Pune – you must be joking" a cardiologist colleague commented. He was responding to a query from my wife as we tried to get-together the nuts and bolts and curtains and maids to assemble a livable house. "We changed 5 maids in the last as many months"- he continued. "We probably would have changed them more often. We were avoiding the hassles of calculating percentage re- numeration".

There is a condition that is common, but not unique to working couples. It has been described in literature as "Tremens domesticus". This occurs usually when a house maid is yet to be employed. It could also occur later. After extracting some loans and wheedling out gifts, a maid could disappear. Often, but not always she would reappear after seeing the sights and attending a couple of matinees. The excuse always was "Mandir gaye" [had gone to the temple]. 'Tremens domesticus' was near its peak on the third day of shifting to our new abode. We spread the word through the servant quarter (gossip) grape vine. The expected queue of aspirants had not obliged by lining up outside our door.

The doorbell rang. My daughter peeped through and ran back all excited. "I think it is a maid – she looks kind of cross – but then I am used to this kind of looks from both of you ". We settled into interview mode and my wife opened the door. I had been instructed to stand in the back ground and look severe. I would play the part of an irascible baba - Wife would do the interviewing.

Shehnaz, was her stated name. She was upward of 50 years old. Yes, she had worked as a maid before, in 'Jamaica' – for five years, before returning to India. Her husband did part time work at the Jai Hind College. She could cook and they had no children. Shehnaz looked clean, but they had no references. Owing to the poverty of competition she was hired. Her husband did a decent job of cleaning up the servant wing of our apartment [the only time I saw him work]. We now had a maid.

Shehnaz was a pleasant surprise in many ways. She was an excellent cook and like many great artists was constantly unhappy on the quantum, quality and variety of raw materials we could provide. She could never be hurried [another artistic trait] and we soon learned the value of pursuing other occupations till she declared "Khana thanda ho raha hai" [the food is getting cold]. This meant in reality that the food was ready.

She mixed her flavors and essences to a nuance. As the meal progressed our ire at having lunch at three would be tempered with appreciation. One could cope with her gripes. May be, life at times had been harsh.

Her husband, Asif, was a mystery. He would dress-up and depart the house early afternoon – to return late at night. Whatever his occupation, it seemed to procure him precious little re-numeration, for he was always extorting money from Shehnaz, she had developed a habit of banking her money in a corner of our kitchen. On Sundays, when she had the afternoon off, she would draw from her booty and set off with her husband for an evening in town and a movie.

She would confide in our daughter of the better times she had. Her husband, it seems was a movie buff and an aspiring film producer to boot. He had a script for a movie ready – songs and all. They were waiting for a break. Asif had a weakness for alcohol. Coupled with his aversion for work, this would have ensured a constant state of penury. Yet he dressed well and drove around on a two-wheeler of dubious vintage. A year after the couple moved into our house he declared to Shehnaz, that he intended to marry again. His new bride to be was a young girl half his age. He assured Shehnaz that he could maintain two households, a sort of modern Krishna. His religion sanctioned him three marriages. He was just following the tenets of the holy book. There were some other tenets.

he chose not to follow- like the one forbidding the use of alcohol. But he had no claims of being perfect. We now came to know that this was his third marriage. The first wife lived with two sons somewhere in Mumbai.

Shehnaz was more withdrawn now. Some of her cocky arrogance was gone. The Sunday outings for movies stopped. Her savings kitty expanded. She did our work and in the day hours, when there was no one at home she would go visiting. Asif's visits to Shehnaz were become very less frequent. When he did come, there would be raised voices and arguments. Then, one day he stopped coming. Shehnaz was now on her own.

Slowly she seemed to get a grip over herself. She was more punctual. She would wake up early and finish the kitchen work with a new efficiency. She dressed neatly now. We wondered what her little secret was. But as she did her work and created no trouble for us, we did not probe too deep.

Two years passed. We were moving out of Pune. We had told Shehnaz about our plans. We offered to find her another home- where she could work. She politely declined. A week before we were to leave, she had a request. She wanted us to have a meal at a small hotel where she had a share.

The place she took us to was small, but neat. It was owned by her brothers and she had put her saving s into it. After we left Pune, Shehnaz would take over the hotels cooking. They had an arrangement with a factory at the outskirts of the city. They would provide the meals for their canteen. This venture had been financed with Shehnaz's capital.

A decade later I visited Pune for a conference. Out a whim I drove down to the old colony where I had once resided. I saw Asif- he was pushing his old scooter. He recognized me. Asif's new wife was working

as a maid in one of the houses. He was still unemployed. He refused to talk about Shehnaz.

I skipped the evening banquet and tried to trace Shahnaz's old hotel. They seemed to have shifted. A new posh hotel had come up in its place. I turned away – but something in the hotels name caught my attention. 'Shehazs'. I went in and ordered dinner. The food was good and the ambience unobtrusive. I sent my credit card to clear the bill. The waiter came back. The hotel owner wanted to see me. I was taken to a room adjacent to the dining hall. There, seated in her executive chair was Shehnaz. Her hairdo had changed and she had an executive demeanour. "Sahib- Khana kaise tha?" she asked. Shehnaz had broken her shackles at last and was free.

*****

The Dog Who Ate Cabbage

Once upon a time we had a dog. We called him Rikki. Rikki was named after the famous mongoose Kipling created in his classic short stories. Rikki was an apso by birth. Initially denizens of Tibet, these puny wonders with their under developed bodies have large thumping hearts full of affection and joy. It is one of the great tragedies of the heart that unstinted affection is often misinterpreted as poor intelligence. With youthful sadism, I made him sniff upturned beetles with sharp pincers. I encouraged him to investigate the whirling spokes of cycles or to charge down garden paths where his poor vision (compounded by his hair falling over his eyes) would cause him to trip over a concealed step and roll over in a muddy football.

Rikki's loyalty never wavered. He would wait for me as I cycled back from school. He could discern the tone of my cycle bell from that of others. He would whelp and prance around announcing joyfully and loudly to the neighbour-hood that the young master had returned. Later when I was away at Pune for my medical education, he would lie distraught on the verandah, cocking up a ear whenever a bicycle passed. In my term breaks when I went home, he would look up enquiringly when my auto-riksha stopped at the gate. His ears would pop up when he heard my voice. A call from me and the six-month absence was forgotten & forgiven in a flurry of licks & a fusillade of joyful whelps. Absence actually made the heart grow fonder, at least amongst the canine species.

Rikki's dietary preferences were unusual to say the least. He relished his morning idli and chutni. He liked tomatoes- sliced with a dash of salt on them. The most remarkable of his dietary nuances was his love for cabbage. He would get up on his hind legs to beg for a sliver of cabbage. He would then carry it into a corner where he would gobble up the morsel with great relish. A genetic or metabolic explanation for his cabbagophilia escapes me to this day.

He was obviously vegetarian only in his dietary habits. He would charge stray dogs who dared venture into our court yard, with wild abandon. Size was no deterrent, even when the strays in question outweighed him by a good 20 pounds, Rikki would charge them with murderous intent. On two occasions we literally rescued him from the jaws of death. Some intolerant stray dogs of unphilosophical disposition did not take

kindly to undergrown pooches charging them whelping profanities.

Once my medical school days were behind me, visits home became less regular. Courses, residencies, and ambition conspired and colluded to keep me away from home. My mother, who was never a dog lover, was finding Rikki more and more of an encumbrance. Rikki restricted her mobility & curtailed her freedom to visit and to be on the move. A solution was desperately needed. Temporary caretakers were initially sought & later Rikki was shifted to foster parents.

A year later when I visited Kerala again, I decided to look up Rikki at his new home. He had been loaned to a distant uncle settling in Kerala after retirement. The couple was gracious. I am confident that Rikki would have been well looked after. The ritual remonstrations on the state of my heath and

nutrition and appreciations of my academic endeavours were over. I could not find Rikki anywhere. It was my uncle who broke the news to me. Rikki had died. He had refused to eat his food and slowly wasted away. I was reminded of the popular song about grand fathers' clock, which stopped- short never to run again after the old man left for a heavenly abode. The dog who ate cabbage had died of a broken heart.

*****

The Fisherman and The Mermaid

There is a fishing hamlet near Cochin called Galilee. We were driving past this colony one Sunday morning. At my mother's insistence, we stopped the car. There was a chapel in this hamlet called Christopher's chapel, where people of all religions and denominations came and prayed for favors. As we reached the chapel Sunday's communion service was over. An old priest, Father Agnes, was with the congregation.

Father Agnes was a kind old soul and he welcomed us with warmth. I was curious of the origin of the church's name and asked father Agnes the obvious question. "Who was Christopher"? "It is a long story", said Father Agnes. "If you will join me for lunch, I will tell you the legend of Christopher". It was nearing lunch hour. We were all fond of sea food. This was the story Father Agnes told.

Chengalam Christopher was a fisherman as had been his father and grandfather before him. They were enterprising and hardworking people, and versed in the vagaries of the ocean and its treasures. They were exploited by the business community as they were uneducated and had no exposure to modern technology. A local missionary had tried to get the fishermen a better deal by bringing in prosperous catholic businessmen as traders. But these men proved even more mercenary and had scant respect for the fishermen or of their traditions. Realizing that educating the fisher folk was the key to their empowerment and emancipation a Christian mission had opened a school for

the fishing villages. A school bus would collect children from five fishing hamlets studded along the coast line. The school provided the children with uniforms and meals. Some political activists had tried to close the school down. They were worried about the Christian influence and even more that the education provided would liberate the fishing community. Middle level businessmen and bankers would loose their easy pickings. The fishermen were however a hardy lot and no political goons were foolish enough to cause trouble in their midst. They understood the wisdom of Father Agnes, then a young missionary, placed in charge of the school. The school started and thrived. A bunch of hired goons who had tried to torch the school and chapel had just disappeared. It was rumored that the fishing folk had fed them to the sharks. No one tried any funny business after that.

Christopher was in his early twenties when the school was started. As a child Chris had helped his mother Kathryn to sort out the fish that the men caught in their fishing boats. They would then go to the depot where the traders would be waiting. There would be the usual round of bargaining before a deal was struck. The traders rarely paid more than a third of the value of the fish. The rest was their profit.

The fisher folk knew the ocean and its seasons. The sea was kind and yielded generously of its treasures. The habitat was prosperous. Yet the ocean could at times be treacherous and unforgiving. Every family had loved ones who had never returned after a night's fishing. At these times the coast guard would be alerted. Search missions would be launched. But the ocean was vast and lost ones rarely found. The sea had its share of predators too. As a kid, Christopher had seen Mustafa return from fishing, his arm chewed off by a tiger shark, the stump dripping blood despite the makeshift tourniquet.

When Christopher was fifteen years old, he had started going out to sea with the fishing boats. Well, built, strong and fearless, he grew up to be a handsome young man. He was enthralled with the ocean and to him fishing expeditions were more than a job to be done.

He was in his element in the blue waters and would often venture out alone with his scoop nets and hooks. An eligible bachelor, quite a few damsels from nearby hamlets had their eyes on him. But Christopher repulsed all proposals and informed the village elders that he was not interested in marriage. The hamlet respected his decision. A mans life was his own and Christopher was a man of honor. The damsels soon turned their attention to more receptive zones.

Monsoons had churned the sea into a murky brown hue. Fishing boats lay idle heeding storm warnings. The fish would have drifted to calmer waters of the deep. Only a few hardened men went out in their one-man canoes to catch some fish to keep the pots boiling. Christopher had ventured out alone, braving the swells. Dusk was rolling in and shoreline had long dipped below the horizon. The face of the moon was hidden by a rigorous purdah of black clouds.

Christopher was just starting to row back when he was startled by a woman's voice from the back of the boat. He turned to see a lady of great beauty sitting in his boat. Her eyes were muddy brown and her jet-black hair was in disarray. Christopher continued to row his boat. All fishermen in the locality knew the legend of the mermaid. She would do no harm. As the lights of the fishing village appeared at the horizon Christopher turned back again. The maid had disappeared, but the empty net he had drawn back into his boat was full of fish. The next evening, she was back in Christopher's boat. The sea was calmer today and the mermaid's demeanour was softer. The monsoon was receding and the sea was getting calmer. The fishing boats ventured out every night. Christopher would however go alone in his boat. Night after night he spend precious time with the damsel of the deep. Her hair was shiny like the oceans surface and her eyes were azure, the color of the deep. She spoke for the first time, her voice calm and serene. "Tell me about your world", she told Christopher, "I see beautiful lights and flying metal birds and ships that are larger than the blue whale. I hear the laughter of men and women, but I sense too a deep unhappiness that runs like a common thread through all this gaiety and laughter".

Christopher was an honest man. "I am not an educated man", he said. "But if you so wish, I will bring you books from father Agnes' school". The next morning Christopher went to father Agnes' school and borrowed a few primary school books. Father Agnes knew that Christopher was illiterate. He liked Christopher and decided to let the mystery unravel itself over time. That evening, at sea in his boat, the mermaid read the books aloud to Christopher. Time stood still for them and their patch of sea was calm and cocooned in a mist of light and haze. Goggle eyed fish popped out of the water all round to listen to the mermaids reading, a couple of dolphins nodded their heads sagely at her words. The mermaid read through all the books and then paused. The mist lifted and she disappeared into the waters.

There was a plop as a shoal of fish landed in his net and dolphins gently nudged the boat back to the shore. Every evening Christopher would bring her new books, on literature and art, geography and geophysics. They read about the beauty and wonders of the universe and of the treachery of men. Father Agnes' library was exhausted and he drew on the monastery library to lend to Christopher. He sensed a miracle in progress and Christopher's erudition amazed him. "Who is it that reads to you, Christopher"? He asked one day. "It is a fair lady of the ocean", Christopher replied. "Do you love this lady", Father Agnes asked. "I love her very much", replied Christopher. "Then why don't you marry her? She is doing you and the fishing village so much of good".

That evening Christopher rowed out to sea again. The mermaids eyes were a deep blue and she wore a white dress shimmering like flitting white topped waves in a moonlit sky. As she read through the 'Poetry of the ages", Christopher looked deeply into her eyes. Her cheeks were flushed now and she paused. "Will you marry me?" Christopher asked her. She seemed to look, through his mind and into his heart for one long long moment. "Yes Christopher", she whispered. There was a flurry of fins as a school of flying fish put an aerobatic display. The dolphins danced, while in the skies overhead shooting stars put up a celebratory pyrrhic display. "Tell father Agnes to be at the beach at midnight ". The mermaid urged Christopher.

Dawn was breaking as Christopher reached the shore. There was a red glow coming from the shoal of fish in his baskets today. Sifting through, he found a fish holding in its mouth, a clam shell purse. Prising it open, he found a beautiful necklace of pearls and an emerald wedding ring. There was a small packet in the purse, with the inscription, "For Father Agnes to build a church". Inside the packet was a red ruby of

immense beauty.

That evening Christopher rowed out to sea to get his bride. Father Agnes and the fishing folk, decked in their finery waited at the beach. It was a full moon night and the waves churned out a rhythmic wedding march as the couple came back to shore. The bride was decked in silver gown studded with sapphire. Father Agnes conducted the wedding ceremony. The hamlet danced and dined late into the night. As the first red beams of the sun crept up the sky, Christopher and his bride returned to his boat. Two dolphins dressed in the finest livery towed the boat which had been magically festooned with lace and jewels. They would reside in the mermaid's palace in the ocean from now on. The villagers never saw Christopher again. The sea was always kind to them, no storm lashed their boats or huts and the hamlet prospered. Father Agnes built a church with the money they got by selling the ruby. On quiet nights, over the calm waters, would drift a melodious voice. "Hush", the elders would tell their children, "It is the mermaid reading to Christopher".

*****

The Frog Who Lived in My Shoe

This is a story from my Pune days. It was a decade and a half ago. Let me introduce myself, I am a neurosurgeon. My hobby is running. I had a couple of finished marathons under my belt and hoped to finish a few more. I lived in a ground floor house in Pune. Every morning, at five, barring Sundays when I try and honor the Sabbath, I would don my running shoes and set out on a ten kilometer jog.

Sweaty shoes have musky odors. In the interest of maintaining marital harmony, I leave my shoes after my run on the portico. Here, with the purifying balm of sun and fresh air, shoes remain fresh.

One morning, as I tried to pull on my shoes, my toe encountered something soft & decidedly squishy within. On with drawing my foot & peeping inside, I saw a pair of angry green eyes staring at me. There was no threat in the stare, just a look of indignant resignation. The look reminded me of the stares Sister Andrews would give me in my third standard when I forgot my home work yet again. With a bit of coaxing and a couple of hard shakes I managed to extricate the occupant, a large frog.

With a hurt look at me Mr. Frog was on his way. He was possibly muttering to himself. The decadence of today's culture which encouraged activities likes recreational running did not amuse him. He hopped over to the ledge and across it into the garden. It was then that I noticed that he had an injured right hind leg which dragged behind without contributing to his hopping. My clinical interest was aroused. But the frog had little faith in the marvels of modern medicine. He might have suspected that my interest in his leg was culinary and not clinical. He hopped on with an awkward grace and firm resolve.

The next morning, he was there again in my shoe. We settled into a routine. I did not grudge him his nights comfort and he tolerated my early morning insomnia. Every night Mr. Frog would heave himself across the portico ledge and snuggle to sleep in my shoe. In the morning, I would wake him up early and see him off to his physiotherapy appointment wherever it was. There was bond between us now and an unwritten code of conduct. In biological terms we could call it a symbiotic relationship.

My daughter had considered my morning running curiously deviant. But frogs fascinated her. May be she had read too many stories about princes under spells. She tried replacing my shoes with hers. But the fit was not right and may be the odors were not inviting enough. We waited for Mr. Frog to come in and settle for the night in the new shoe. He hopped over the ledge – examined the new shoe with scorn and hopped back again. He disappeared into the thicket. He was later seen drinking away his sorrows at the loss of a familiar home. We tried no further experiments. My shoe was there every night for him from then on. Mr. Frog and I returned to our regular routines.

One windy September morning, I woke up all ready to pound the pavement. As I lifted my shoe, I sensed something amiss. The extra weight of Mr. Frog was not perceptible. I peeped in, turned the shoe down and tapped it firmly – all to no avail. Mr. Frog was not inside. I ran that day with a heavy heart. I wondered what predator had made a morsel of my frog. It might have been a rat snake. I mentally struck off rat snakes from my birthday invitation list. I would have called up the snake association chairman and blasted him, but I did not have his telephone number. May be my frog had been run over by an automobile. I remembered a sign posted at a golf course. Drive carefully to avoid crushing frogs. I did tend to drive a little fast. Surely I haven't. 'NO- I did not remember any squelches'.As my shoe remained unoccupied night after night my worst fears seemed true. Only the perpetrator of the crime remained a mystery. I offered a mental obituary for my departed cohabitant. Then one evening, I saw him again. The frogs' leg was still dragging a bit- but could now add pep to his hop. Hi- hello- I called –but he ignored me. I realized that I and my shoe had been a mere convenience for him during a period of disablement. I no longer mattered. To the frog, it had just been an arrangement of convenience. How human!!!!!

*****

# The Lion and the Hunter

John-De-Cruz was the General Manager of Unicorn Breweries. He was a good man and a solid and responsible citizen. He was regular at Church, religious in his convictions, unshakable in his integrity and unfailing in his social obligations. He was also an excellent Manager. With diligence, hard work, industry, and unshakable honesty, he had turned the failing United Breweries around in the past 10 years. Researching, revising, and streamlining the processes from harvest to distillation and distribution of the quality spirits; he achieved this miracle. Consumers had started to expect and received quality products from the company. He gave discourses at management institutes on the technique of clean and efficient management. He was the President of the local chapter of the Rotary Club. His wife and children had a grouse. They had not had a holiday for as long as they could remember. John like many perfectionists abhorred the idea of handing over the reins of control to another. There was a fear that in his absence someone could ruin the well-oiled system by inaction or by ill-advised initiative.

John's wife took matters into her hands one day and button holed the company owner. Mr. Sorabhji appreciated the efforts of John in achieving the turnabout in the company he had inherited. "John needs a break", his wife told Sorabji. If he keeps on at this pace, he will soon crack up. Sorabji was a good man. He agreed totally with John's wife. He would work out the modalities in a month.

Mr Sorabji arranged a business meet at Kenya with a sister concern, after which John and his family were to stay back for a safari. With only a bit of reluctance John agreed. His family needed a holiday. It was an offer too good to refuse. He told his wife to get-together the binoculars, bermudas, brown safari outfits & broad rimmed hats befitting the expedition. A month later the De-Cruz family was in Kenya. The business meet was perfunctory. Soon afterward they were bundled into a Land Rover with an African guide and were heading deep into the African forest.

By the end of the week, they had criss-crossed the more frequented parts of the beaten trail. They had encountered herds of elephants and Zebras, got close to grazing giraffes and got chased by an irate rhinoceros. The land rover roared from jungle to clearing to sending gaggles of wild birds to flight. At night they would camp out in the open. They would sit around the fire watching myriad fire flies putting up a pyrrhic display. The stars were brighter than any they had seen in city life. The family would then retire into their tents for protection from mosquitoes and flies. Mornings would see them fresh and ready. They would head out into the African Savannah in a little whirl wind of brown dust. They were however yet to see a lion.

John decided to press on further into the unexplored Jungle. The safer parts of the jungle had already been explored. The forest stretched deep beyond the border of the Safari. The guides warned the Cruzs against venturing further. There was a rogue lion out there. He was called Sumbero by the locals. Sumbero meant the Devil and he had earned his name. He had made a meal of a missionary couple and mauled a score of locals. John tapped his Winchester rifle – If Sumbero materializes, he said – I will be ready.

John's short service stint in the Army had armed him with a certain skill with a rifle. To his mind Sumbero was just another industrialist who might attempt a hostile takeover. The modern day Rambo and his entourage headed into Sumbero country, dense uncharted jungle. That night they camped in a clearing in the forest. The dull glow from red ambers of the campfire did not detract from the brilliant display put up by the stars and meteors in a moonless sky. The serenity of the jungle was suddenly shattered by a lion's roar. In a trice De-Souza had his loaded Winchester on his shoulder and he fired. They could hear the noises of a large creature heading away through the undergrowth. That was Sumbero – whispered their shaken guide. The camp was rolled up hastily and the adventurers headed back to the safer confines of the reserve forest. The Rangers had heard the shot and were relieved when the Decruzs rolled in. Family and friends complemented Cruz on his quick thinking and ready reflexes. My dad is like Rambo, his daughter whispered – her dark eyes shining with admiration. Sumbero had been the undisputed King of that Kenyan forest. Huge and mangy, he had been leader of his pride. Then one day he had get his paw caught in a hunters trap. Lamed and lonely, he hunted alone. He could no longer out sprint the fleet footed antelope. With his size and strength he could get a slower water buffalo that ventured too close. The occasional missionary for a meal reflected his anger at humanity in general. Sumbero had spotted the De-Cruz's and as they set up camp in his backyard. Padding noiselessly closer he was hardly 5 paces away from the large bald man, who carried a rifle. Sumbero saw the rifle and recognized it for what it was. It did not trouble him. The kill would be over before the bald man could raise his fire stick. He crouched – ready to spring.

Suddenly an angel materialized in front of him. He recognized Gabriel. He was reminded of the sound thrashing he had received from Gabriel after he had raided the missionary camp. Sumbero slunk away – his tail between his legs – he knew when he was beaten. As he padded away into the undergrowth – he roared in frustration – for he was hungry. It was at the sound of his roar that commotion broke out in the camp – a shot was fired. Sumbero was already a safe distance away. But something else had been hit. A wounded water buffalo shuffled across his track. Sumbero smiled to himself, Gabriel had ensured that Sumbero would not go hungry tonight.

Gabriel returned to his heavenly abode – De-Cruz thinks he scared Sumbero away –

he confided in St. Peter. Yes – agreed St. Peter – humans are vain.

*****

The Snake

Pine apple groves attract snakes. This is village wisdom. Such observations, although lacking scientific validation, are true nevertheless. My father, the inhouse herpetologist (also local political analyst, philosopher and sports critic) opined that the sharp spines on the pineapple leafs helped the snakes molt their skins. Prickly leaves prevented other animals from straying in to the patch, providing a safe haven for the snakes. Walking across the pineapple grove in the dark was unwise. Visits to check on the ripeness of the fruit were undertaken with circumspection.

The grove required tending. Young fruits had to be wrapped in a protective calyx of the spiny leaves. These were held in place by cords stripped off the trunk of banana trees. Birds and rats were kept at bay.

Weeds had to be cut, the hedge needed trimming.

Kannan, our gardener had been once greeted by the spread hood of a menacing cobra when he pried among the leaves to check the fruit. Being well versed in the behavior of snakes, he stood still. The cobra lowered its hood and slithered away. My daughter Shreya, all of eight years of age had ventured into the grove during her holidays. A snake wrapped itself around her leg. Not being versed in snake lore and possibly lacking Kannan's courage, she stood and screamed till the bemused snake slid away for a quiet chuckle with his friends.

Our relationship with the pine apple grove snakes was based on mutual respect. There was no occasion where they transgressed into our living space. Whenever we ventured into the grove, we gave them ample warning. We would stomp our feet as we walked into the grove. Snakes, devoid of a separate hearing apparatus depended on their perception of vibrations to identify danger.

Once a snake realized that you were heading their way, they would generally move away.

With snakes guarding the patch we were spared from rats. Our tapioca plantation was undisturbed from rats gnawing at the tubers. Family clusters of banana trees dotted the courtyard; seasonal flowerings of the mango tree would give a bonanza of fruit which we shared with visiting birds and relatives. It was a veritable Garden of Eden replete with snakes and succulent fruit.

Over a period of time, we had a rough estimate of the identity of our snake population. Ka- the cobra was rarely seen- but his presence was always felt. He lived in a mud hole behind a termite hill. The gateway to his castle was shielded by the branches of a partially uprooted mango tree which failed to hold its own against a monsoon blast. In another corner two rat snakes could be seen cavorting or basking for a sun tan. A green tree snake lived on an old mango tree and would occasionally be seen in the shrubbery and the hedge. A few small snakes of unknown vintage, like the one which had wrapped itself around my daughters' leg completed the list. Every year before winter set in, a carpet of mushrooms would cover the garden with their white umbrellas.

Then, one day my father had a heart attack. Complaining of chest pain, he was shifted to the local medical college. My father survived the attack but, on the cardiologists, advice shifted base to a flat in town and nearer medical care. Our house in the village relegated to the position of a weekend resort. The garden still bloomed, but weeds over ran the paths. The hedges were no longer trimmed and leeching saprophytes sucked the life out of the mango trees. A few petty thieves eyed the pineapples but Kannan during the day and Ka at night kept them at bay.

The stalemate in the garden was resolved by political intervention. One of the petty thieves was also a political activist. He was often called in by the party when buses needed to be stoned, shop window panes broken, skulls cracked, or other democratic indulgences deemed necessary for the preservation of liberty were exercised. The local legislator was called in to study the snake menace in the vicinity. A political tout called on my father offering to abort the move, for a price. My father refused.A snake hunt was organized by the local panchayat protected by a few pan chewing policemen. A harmless rat snake, lazing in the sun was thrashed to death. A photograph of the legislator standing over the dead snake, with an up raised stick made it to the page 2 of the local daily. As the photograph appeared next to the matrimonial column it was widely appreciated. The legislator received many accolades and two marriage proposals. Pine apples disappeared, as did mangoes, a petticoat hung out for drying by our maid servant and the bronze name plate at our gate.

The snakes were never seen again, nor the birds. The pineapple plants did not bloom and the mango trees did not flower. The mushrooms never materialized again. The Garden of Eden had died with the snakes.

****

The Street Urchin And The Almonds

It was a hot summer afternoon at Pune & I was driving on a departmental errand. At the Pool-gate crossing. I stopped for a red light, spotted a traffic cop before he could glance in my direction & quickly fastened my seat belt. Three was a tap on the glass pane at the passenger window. A street urchin stood with his nose flattened on the glass & an imploring look in his eyes. I rolled down the glass halfway & parted with a coin to this demi-official toll collector. But today the toll collector did not seem satisfied. He kept pointing at dash board and I could soon decipher that he was saying badam. I looked in the direction he pointed. There, on the dash my daughter had forgotten her almonds – wrapped up in a piece of tissue which had fluttered half open.

I handed him the little collection & edged the car forward as the signal lights had turn green. I watched him scamper to the side to share the spoils with an even more decrepit looking little girl. The frisky joys of child hood were barely muted by poverty. The deprived find happiness in simple comforts. Rich kids are unhappy and more difficult to please. The spontaneity and values of these kids was immaculate. Child labour stifled joys of childhood. Poverty did not. I could not help contrasting street kids with the children employed in beedi rolling or carpet making. The rigor and responsibility of labour and earning invoked in them a discipline and purpose. This discipline would stymie and be inimical to the joyous exuberance of childhood.

There are lobbies of committed individuals & organizations of repute engaged in parlays and engrossed in the merit of legislation on child labour and on assuaging the agonies of homeless poverty. While they commit themselves to debates, let us follow the evolution and travails of our street urchin.

The story of our urchin is embroiled in the ethos of a beggar's world with its corporatised cruelty. Our urchin and his friends were the property of a controller who deployed them across the city in the mornings and would swoop them up to harvest their pickings by sundown. All the kids could keep was the occasional pinch of almonds wrapped in tissue.

The urchin boy grew – as boys usually do. His controller started wising of to the fact that the urchin was as you might say straining at his leash. That, and the fact the urchin's personality was evoking a following amongst the younger ones caused the controller consternation. Loyalties and friend ship did not figure in his vision or fit into his grand scheme or design. He started planning to cripple the urchin. A handicapped beggar was aa asset. Blind or Lame, he would evoke a human-interest appeal. Coupled with an emotive magnetism, he would be a hit in crowded recreational zones especially in the holiday season. Handicapping him would also curtail any consideration of rebellion in the ranks. The controller was a genius.

Our urchin sensed impending catastrophe. He was less that eager to sacrifice his eyes or a limb to the ' cause. Drawing upon his intuitive brilliance and capitalising on his superior knowledge of battle zone terrain, the urchin escaped. He evaded the hired henchmen awash with malignant intent. He hopped on a locomotive heading to Mumbai. This is where he planned to make his own fortune. The journey however got prematurely terminated. Less than half way to Mumbai, nearing Khandala station, a conscientious ticket examiner accosted him. The inspectors sentiment against ticket less travel was conveyed to the urchin through the hard toe of his uniform shoe.

A cold mist hung over the platform as the urchin evaluated his new abode. The Khandala platform, he realized, was already taken. His eyes scanned the platform. Little beggars were scouring the platform for easy pickings. His trained eye spotted too – the handler – super visioning the harvest with cool efficiency. A cold head of sweat broke out on the urchin's forehead. The handlers he knew were not averse to enforced on the spot recruitment. They could and would pick up unattended children to bolster their regiments. This one looked particularly nasty and was looking in his direction. There was no time to be lost.

An elderly gentleman was struggling with his suitcase. 'Sahib- 2 rupiah keliya may baksa apke gaddi taak pahuncha dunga' (for two rupees I will carry the suitcase to your car). Mr. Kataria, an elderly civil retired civil servant was the sahib in question & he suffered from gout, sciatica, haemorrhoids and hubris. He shared the morbid fear of all government officials of cancer, consumerism, communism & constipation – not necessarily in that order. His driver Sadhu Ram was late yet again & the suitcase was heavy. The suitcase was loaded on the urchin's head and they made their way to the parking lot.

Outside the station, the urchin clung on to the box. Kataria pondered the possibility of his old fiat car developing the wheezes as it often did on cold winter mornings. He sensed the potential need for this young porter to carry the box to the auto stand. His irate consternation resulted in an extension of the urchins employment.

Fifteen minutes had passed – the urchin had procured a hot cup of elaichi tea for the irate gentleman. The elaichi in the tea make Kataria benevolent. He asked the urchin. "Kahan raheta hai tu" (where do you stay). "I have come from the village" lied the urchin. "There is no work there and the draught has withered the winter crop".

 "Will you work our garden" – Kataria was being impulsive- "Kuch chori karega to tera nak kat dunga" (if you steal something we will cut off your nose). Mr. Kataria was an impulsive man. He drove through life on instinct & judgement which were both sound. These evolved instincts had served him shabbily in the civil services. In government service sycophancy & conformity with the system were extolled virtues. Kataria retired as an assistant commissioner, while his intellectually inferior colleagues attained appointments of glamour and influence. Devoid of intellectual sparks they rendered offices impotent. Opportunities were frittered away by paucity of imagination.

Peep – the familiar horn of the Fiat interrupted. Mr. Kruminations. There was a ritual of remonstration as he chided Sadhu Ram on the perils of being unpunctual. Kataria then informed him that the urchin had been hired as a live-in gardener. He would sleep in the out-house and use the garden toilet. Sadhu Ram was entrusted with his tutelage. Sadhu Ram was suspicious of the urchin but his boss's ire had been recently aroused. Debate and discussion could re kindle the fire – he acquiesced.

That is how the urchin, whose name was Ravi come to the Kataria house. He tended the garden and in time was taught to drive the Fiat. A neighbourhood lady repaid her moral debt and fulfilled her social obligations (which she had neglected for 30 yrs as a teacher and later as headmistress of a hill station school), by tutoring Ravi and two other local servants, in reading and writing in English and the vernacular.

Ravi carted the Kataria clan sight serving around Khandala. When the Kataria boy came home on holiday from Harward law school, he drove him around and to Mumbai for friendship and courtship. When Mr Kataria fell ill, he shuttled daily from Khandala to the Riviere hospital in Mumbai. His street credentials helped him negotiate with the bevy of sub specialties eager to sink their stethoscopes into a piece of Katarias insurance pie. Disseminated prostatic cancer ultimately caught up with Mr Kataria.

Ravi mourned his loss as deeply as any in the family. A distraught Mrs Kapadia was taken by her son to the United Kingdom to grace the Tudor house, which the younger Kataria had acquired at Leicester. Ravi was appointed the charge –de – affairs of Kataria's Indian interests. Despite their obvious prosperity and acceptance in the English social circles and the younger and brighter Katarias betrothal to a British School teacher, they were loathe the sever the link or may be the safety net of their origin where street urchins were blinded for begging and where rail tracks doubled as public toilets.

They put up capital for Ravi to set up a departmental store. As manager of the Kataria interest's at Khandala & Pune he was answerable by e- mail & received monthly remittances from the elder of the Kataria kin.

As Ravi prospered, he made one undercover expedition to Pune- culminating in the rescue of his urchin girl friend. She was by then prepared for initiation to a local brothel by their controller. The story of the rescue is mumbled in hushed whispers by the urchins of Pune to this day. Suffice to say that they managed to board a Mumbai bound train, this time with tickets & reached the safety of the Kataria estate. The couples wedding was blessed by the local gentry & again by the Katarias who contributed a car- Maruti -800 to the happy couple.

A decode went by, the Ravis shifted to Pune to supervise the inceasing Kataria investment in real estate, including a lucrative partnership in an evolving colony for NRIs.

The Ravi couples son attended the Harchongs School & was a prefect in his 8th class. They were returning from a PTA meet, where Mrs. Ravi was an office bearer when the traffic signal turned red at the Pool gate junction. As the car stopped – an urchin ambled up, tapping at the passenger window & pointing beseeching at a half action packet of biscuits on the car's dash board. Drat those urchins-cursed Ravi, as he engaged gears & sped away.

****

Future War

The lights blinked again. Mustafa wrinkled his forehead in irritation. The intellectual subversion of the empire was nearing completion. The infidels who prepared for unconventional war had been woefully off the mark. It had taken the group a century of subversive effrontery to achieve their aim. Mustafa himself had been initiated into the echelons thirty years ago. He was fortunate to be in the final phase and experience the fruition. Impatiently he fiddled with the TV's controls. The news channels were predictably friendly. There had been a subtle paradigm shift in threat perception. It was now the ultraconservatives and neo-rightists who

 posed a threat to stability. The group had set the media as an early and prime target for infiltration.

There was something in the news that caught his attention. A renegade scholar had written a book on the intellectual-economic subversion of Europe. The book had been banned the world over as subversive. These were the perils of power. It had been easier to hoist themselves into a position of control. To maintain the order would need a new dynamic. Phase three would have to be initiated soon, or they would end up with same decadent collapse as the democratic empires of Europe.

He wished Ameena and the children would come home. There was loneliness in his fulfilment, an uneasy angst that would be assuaged by the balm of domesticity. Mustafa heard the buzz as the electronically controlled gates opened. He zapped the TV off. The front door opened and the girls came running in. They were twins, Sabina and Sahiba. Twelve years ago, when they were born, Ameena had been a burqa clad housewife. They had at that time scouted the length and breadth of Paris to locate an obstetric department with an all-woman team. Today Ameena preferred trendy western outfits.

Sabina was coming towards him holding something furry in her hands. He could see Ameena glance nervously from the kitchen door. Mustafa had always been wary of dogs. He remembered the time when the old French democratic regime brought in austerity measures to salvage their sinking economy. Mustafa and his friends had infiltrated the workers movement and braved rubber bullets and water cannons of the police forces. The police dogs had once chased Mustafa over a wall and along the river bank till he finally jumped into the water to escape them. Mustafa's fear of dogs was possibly his only weakness. He looked at the puppy in his daughter's hands and again into her imploring eyes. In a year the pup would grow into a full-grown dog and would be all over the house. He knew that he should take a stand before it was too late. The victories of the past had softened him. He smiled at his daughter. She ran to hug him.

He was lost in thought. There was a time when he would have never compromised. He had lost some battles, but the war had been won. The Americans had held out the longest. The swing in public opinion had been overwhelming. After all it was a democracy and no leader could hold out for long against public will.

The girls had moved on into their room. Mustafa could hear squeals of enjoyment as they experienced their new acquisition. Ameena was stealing glances at him from the kitchen door. It was time for her favourite soap show. It was time he returned to his room and his books. He rose. The family would get together for dinner in an hour. He wondered if the others in the group had grown equally soft. The intensity of commitment had evaporated and decadence had set in over all of them. With a sigh he realised that it too late for phase three.

A JOURNEY

Tulsidas Karamchand steeled himself for the interview. He had prepared for this moment for years. He felt curiously light headed. He had been with the company for over two decades. With every passing year the ethos had become more stifling.

Mumbai airport had evolved. He had booked himself tickets on an economy carrier. As he indulged himself with an overpriced Pepsi at the food court, he marvelled at the sophisticated exuberance of the terminal and the immaculate efficiency of the airline ground staff. He had flown to Brussels on company business a while ago and marvelled at the expanse and experience of their international airport. Today Bombay's international domestic airport seemed comparable. We had come a long way.

There was a slight delay in the flight schedule. The President was in town for a state visit and commercial flights were stalled till his aircraft took off. Then it was time to board. They jostled down the proboscis to the aircrafts belly, where he squeezed himself into a cramped seat between a flamboyantly flatulent cleric and a woman of imperial proportions. The aircraft engines were humming now as they waited for a window of opportunity to sail off into the dark skies. On the main runway ahead, brilliantly painted cylinders of steel hurtled at inordinate speeds snapping their umbilical cords of gravity in a frenetic desire for flight. Through his window he could see angry reds and beckoning blues, beacons of guidance in the damping darkness of a moonless night. He would have preferred to fly during the day, but the company's policy on leave was stifling. There had been a time when he would have considered any leave an indulgence. This was before his morale succumbed to the constant buffeting of office politics. The administrators stifled them by instilling a desire to excel and then rationing opportunity.

They were in the air now, ears popping in protest at estrangement from terra firma.

The lights of Mumbai coastline receded beneath them. There was some turbulence as they submerged into the inky shrouds of a cloudy sky. It was different in the daytime. It was less alarming. Suspended in the sublime opalescence of billowing clouds mentored by the suns rays one developed a sense of unreality, of transgressing fairyland.

The attendants were carting around food and drinks for sale. There was no interaction with fellow passengers. One would expect certain camaraderie, suspended in isolated companionship thirty thousand feet above the ground, but there was none. Train travel was more relaxed. There was time to unwind and to make friends.

The seat belt sign was on again. Silver spangles of Madras city inlaid with goblets of gold were at the horizon. In the distance, veiled flashes of lightning heralded an incoming monsoon. Gardens of iridescent indicator lights accorded them a Christmassy welcome as they landed with a thud, bounced and then steadied, roaring down the landing strip.

It was drizzling outside and the bus to the terminal was packed to discomfiture. Tulsi had no checked in luggage. He glanced around him as he walked around puddles to the local station, breathing in the sounds and flavour of a new city, with it's unfamiliar ethos and culture and an alien language. He would adapt and make a mark. Tulsi could not afford to fail again.

*****

THE END GAME

Chidambaram was dying. With two cancers at seventy years of age, he had had plenty of time to prepare for this moment. Tanku the maid walked in, with a tray of medicines and a glass of water. Tanku had been with the family all her life. He remembered her as a little girl in a pony tail who swept the courtyard and stole mangos from the basket, where they were kept in soft beds of hay for ripening. He had been a little monkey in his youth, scampering up and down mango trees and swinging precariously from the high branches. Those were the days when the garden lay trimmed and the mango trees gave fruit in abundance. The soil had been rich and as fertile as his unfettered imagination. The trees had aged

now and after his fathers demise had pinned away to obsolescence. Chidambaram looked out of his window. The overgrown carpet of untrimmed vegetation was depressing. Wasted opportunities had culminated in the exuberant shrubbery of inconsequence. As the garden withered, weeds had flourished. Nature abhorred a vacuum.

Chidambaram's house was on a hill and from his window he could see the road to town and the rows of houses on both sides. The landscape had evolved reflecting the state's new ethos. Gone were the endless coconut groves and mud houses with thatched roofs. Brightly coloured little cement houses financed by overseas remittances, painted in colours of defiance now dotted the countryside. Tanku left after making sure that he swallowed his pills. His bravado had long evaporated and the pills were necessary to keep away the pain. He knew he was dying long before Dr Mathur studied the MR images with the gravity of an undertaker and proclaimed that the cancer was incurable. He had felt the malignancy gnaw at his bones before the technetium scan picked up hot spots of activity. Cancer cells had taken over the controls. No knife or clever manipulation of metabolic differences could eke them out. The medications offered a welcome respite from the agony. They numbed his senses, but at this stage it really did not matter.

It was Sunday today and a trickle of well wishers would drop in. Sundays used to be fun days when he was a kid. Attending church was mandatory. He and the other children squatted on the floor in the first three rows, boys and girls in two groups on either side of a central passage. Giggling during service was taboo and to glance at the girls invited sure-fire divine retribution. Later during the Sunday school hour, he would look surreptitiously at the girls, their complexions creamed with fairness potions. This was where he had fallen in love with fair and long limbed Renuka who stood a good half foot taller than him. He would crane his neck around the contorted trunks of gnarled coconut trees to look at her. He could never actually speak to her, but this was Kerala where the sexes interacted only behind the closed doors of matrimony.

His breakfast was being brought in now. For the past month he had been too weak to sit at the table with the rest of the family. His grandchildren would be making a ruckus with their endless squabbles. Chidambaram's presence would dampen everyone's spirits. Tanku propped him up against the pillows and spread a towel on his lap over which she placed the food tray. He would eat slowly over the next hour and then she would clean up and offer him a mug of water to rinse his mouth out.

As a young man, Chidambaram had a hearty appetite. He would polish off mountains of rice and curry before waiting, smacking his lips for the payasam. He would burn it all of on the mudbanks of the Meenachil river which was their football field. The air had been clean and pure those days, freshened by life giving puffs from the three oceans around the tip of the Indian peninsula. Even the mud had been cleaner those days, wholesome, life-giving, soggy and earthy. There was a rubber plantation nearby, where he could run to his hearts content. He had loved running even then, leaping nimbly over the protruding roots, feeling the wind in his ears. There could be snakes under the carpet of dry leaves, but as a child he had no fear, the belief in his own invincibility had been absolute. His courage had been tempered with time and the fear of failure and ridicule had plagued him in his later years, but that was the price of success in today's world. Some of the optimism had never faded, thought Chidambaram with a smile. He winced as a sharp stab of pain shot down his side. His fate never let him brag. He muttered a prayer of contrition as the pain faded away. He would need to step up the dose of morphine soon. The pain, when it hit him was too intense. He lost his appetite. The flashes of pain did that to him. There was remorse within as he fathomed all the unfinished things he had wanted to complete, so much more that he wanted to do. Maybe he would come out of all this unscathed, cheat death for a while. Chidambaram smiled at his own foolishness.

He was pushing optimism to the point of perversion.

There was a time when he had indulged himself in Fiction writing. It helped him to vent his thoughts. Getting published however was a different issue. It had taken him a while to realise that the cold drafts he felt did not herald a flock of penguins flocking to his door. As he faded into insignificance, his writing had lost its relevance and he could no longer capture anyone's imagination.

"Wake up", Tanku was shaking him. He had drifted off to sleep and spilt some of his cereal. She would have to change the bed sheets and his pyjamas. He wanted to apologize for the nuisance, but did not. It was not his fault that he had cancer.

It had been different ten years ago when he had been first diagnosed to have oral cancer. He had an overwhelming sensation of having betrayed his friends, a guilt at not being able to pull his weight, having to draw from the good will and resources he would rather continue to contribute to. He went through the surgery and chemotherapy bravely, but then had got the double whammy of developing a second malignancy in his lung. Two more operations and a decade of hospital-based care had eroded the mantle. "He would be darned if he would apologize". He had seen it all. The callous indifference of young consultants who would send him off on wild goose chases with a bevy of unnecessary tests, the inordinate hurry of middle level nurses who had to rush home from their shift to cook and care for their families and the jealous curiosity of other patients relatives as to why he was getting more attention than them. In the end, the hospital had thrown up its hands. There was nothing that they could do for him except to give him morphine and antiemetics. This could well be done at home. He had been bundled off, unwanted, to wilt away on his own bed, his death sentence irrevocable.

Another pang of pain shot through his leg. He groaned as he felt the bubbles gushing out of his chest. Tanku screamed as the frothy brew bubbled out of his nose and mouth to the freshly laundered sheets. Others came running in, but he could no longer see them. They waited, hands over their mouths, watching the last throes of a dying man.

A little while later, a bed sheet was drawn over his head. Tanku would clean him up and prepare him for his last journey to the grave. They dabbed their red eyes with their white handkerchiefs as they consoled each other. Chidambaram's travails were finally assuaged in the dark shroud of death's embrace.

THE SURGEON

Siddhartha was unwell. He had been noted to be out of sorts for almost a year now. It was during the harvest festival, when the youth had gathered round the ceremonial fire that Siddhu, as he was fondly addressed by villagers, had his first seizure. There was impromptu wrestling match which Siddhu along with other adolescent friends had organized. Siddhu's friend Tambe had Ramane from nearby Tathi village pinned on the grass. The village youth cheered loudly. It was then that his friends noted that Siddhu was in a sort of trance, he sat by the side with a staring & glassy look in his eyes. All of a sudden Siddhu fell down on the grass, his body seemed to tense like a young bamboo rod in the monsoon breeze before going into a series of spasms. There was froth coming from his mouth & a trickle

of blood ran down the side of his cheek. Women screamed in terror- his young friends drew back in confusion. Only Kathi –

the village midwife seemed to know what to do. She, with help from the village lads – pulled him away from the campfire, where they sprinkled water on his face. Siddhu's spasms had now ceased & he seemed to have lapsed into a trance – his breathing was regular but deep & noisy & his eyes were closed. They tried to rouse him – but he was in a slumber as deep as that of Ranial the local drunk after a spree of toddy drinking. He awoke shortly, his eyes opened & he started moving his hands & legs – Sidhu groaned. His friend carried him to his hut & laid him on the floor where he drifted to sleep again. Let him be – said Kathi – she knew that the best thing to do in the circumstance was to let him sleep. If he seizured again – he would possibly die – but there was little she or any of the villagers could do. The nearest medicine man was at Panchtantra, two days away by bullock cart. In the court of the emperor there were physicians who were well versed in the arts of healing – but Delhi was a week journey.

As Kathi predicted, Sidharth woke up the next morning, with a head ache– blissfully amnesic of the tumultuous events of the previous night. He was taken in the bullock cart caravan with part of the village crop for sale to the township of Panchtantra. The fakir listened intently to the description then of events with the burnishing and garnishing provided by Sidhu's uncle. A few questions were asked including the details of a pussing ear what Sidhu had suffered for 3 years but what resolved almost 3 months ago. A detailed Physical examination followed, with Sidhu stripped to his loin cloth."There is an impurity in his head – what need to be let out" – the Fakir opined. I knew of only man who is capable to doing this miracle –the great guru Sushrutha – but to the best of my knowledge he has retired to the great mountains in search of the highest one". There was a certain herb to numb the effect of the impurity and to prevent further convulsions. The Fakir instructed the boy's uncle on where to obtain the herb and how it was to be administered.

Sidhartha returned to the village. He would take cattle to graze and herd them back to their enclosure in the village at sunset. The day would be spent in the green valley by the river bed – the river which separated the village and the grazing land of the village cattle from the dense forest. He carried the herb Sumbrotha – with him – as he went cattle herding. Sumbrotha initially made him sleepy but in the time he got used to the herbs. The herb prevented him from having the kind of attack that occurred during the harvest festival. However, his head aches persisted. He wished to go to the mountains in search of Sushrutha – but the distance (the journey would take him a month) and the fact that the cattle needed him kept him back. Six months after his convulsive attack Sidhu got an opportunity to visit Panchtantra again. The Fakir recognised him from the door and examined him in detail. The impurity was growing, the Fakir concluded – there were signs which his experienced clinical sense could detect. There was subtle stiffness in the right hand and leg & an excessive jumpiness of one side as he tapped some nerve points. When he scratched sole of the foot with a quill, the toe would point toward the imparity (this was a sign his master had demonstrated to the Fakir & to his trained mind – the sign was infallible). Sidha would need Sushrutha's help or it was only a matter of months before his right side would be paralysed & his speech would cease. With all the herbs at his disposal, he could, but delay Sidhus death only by a few more weeks. He liked Sidhartha & wished he could do something for him. A fellow Fakir who made periodic expeditions to the great mountain, in the search for new herbs with medicinal value was leaving for the mountains soon. The Fakir send word to him to tell the great master – if he could be met, about Sidhus melody.

Sidhartha returned to the village. His headaches were worse. Village folk noticed that he dragged his left foot as he returned at dusk with the cattle. He was needing to take larger & larger amount of Sumbrotha &

this would make him sleep through much of the day.

Winter had set in & the mist that rolled in from the forest would lift late in the day – sometimes by late afternoon. He awoke one afternoon from his slumber to hear the lowing of a calf – the cry of an animal in pain or in danger. Clutching his staff he walked through the mist to the river bed. Balu the white calf had waded into the marshy river bed & was stuck. His struggles made him drift deeper into the muddy sludge & the murky flowing water was only a few meters away. A fully grown animal could have freed himself & returned to safety, but Balu was still a calf. The rest of the herd watched - unable to help. Sidhu waded into the water plodding the river bed with staff – identifying the firm patches which would take his weight till he reached the trapped animal. With his staff he found what he was looking for – a patch of firm rock under the soft mud. Sidhu pushed & cajoled the trapped animal toward the firmer ground. At last Balu was free. He tried to lift Balu to his shoulder, but his illness seemed to have sapped his strength. Balu slipped from his grip – but his scrabbling feet encountered the rocky under path Sidhu had sensed. With a frightened leap the animal made it to safe ground & scampered back to the safety of his herd. Sidhu's strength had been drained by the struggle & the Sumbrotha was making him disoriented. He tried to walk back to the shore, but slipped into the murky river, and a sharp current carried him to mid river & then along to the opposite shore.

Barely conscious he paddled with his hand to keep his face above water, but the effort seemed too much – the river current was too strong & he felt the waters close over his head. A hand reached out through the water, under his neck to lift his face out of the water. Strong hands lifted him and carried him to a clearing in the forest. Sidhu was barely able to open his eyes.

He saw two young men in either side of him. They were drying out his soaked clothes & applying a warm oil on his body. By their side stood a lady with a bowls & a shiny white cloth in her hands. These were surely Gods – Sidhu mused. He looked above his head & saw a bearded old man. His face was furrowed by the worries of many moons & a million experiences. Yet his eyes were calm & serene, pools of blue peace in a rugged country side. It is him alright the old man, muttered Fakir Rohila was right – we do not have much time. The lady was asking him to drink from the bowl. It was milk laced with a sweet nectar. It had a kind of sweetness that tickles the senses & calms the mind. Sidhartha slipped into a deep slumber.

Slowly Sidharthas eye fluttered open. There was something different about the world – he realized his headache was gone – the mist from the forest had cleared. The red haze of the setting sun sent fluffs of pink reminiscence to the havering clouds. The cattle were getting restless. Sidhartha rose & with his call he gathered together the straying head. As he walked back to the village, he noticed that his foot no longer dragged. The cattle were safely returned to their enclosure. "What is that on your head", Urmila his sister asked. A glue of leaves was stuck to one side of his head. Sidhu know what had happened – the great master Surgeon had answered the call – Sidhartha was cured.

****

The Spider Who Loved Me

I grew up in Kerala in a house of bricks & country plaster with baked earthen tiles for a roof. As is usual, in these houses, an encyclopedia of insects lived in the cracks & crevices. And most notably there were hordes of spiders. Spiders were everywhere, spindly legged dudding long legs, hairy miniature one's wiry hunters & large black spiders, the size of a sunflower in full bloom.

Spiders frightened me, I had read in country western's that the black widow spiders were more poisonous than a rattle snakes. The pastor in church portrayed hell as an abode of spiders & vipers amidst the fire and friendly. So, an unhealthy bias against spiders had been sort of encoded in my genome. My nightly prayer ended with an incantation for protection from these creatures.

One of the primary duties of our maid, Mary was to keep the population of spiders in check. This she did, with gusto- aided by a coconut leaf broom and a powerful right arm swing which could have done Stephi Graph proud. But the smart spiders survived. They had an uncanny knack of disappearing into some inaccessible crevasse before the broom & its wielder could be alerted.

The fact that I was yet to encounter anyone who had suffered poisoning or injury due to a spider bite. The geo-bio-logical fact that Black widow spiders did not colonise Soult Kerala were factors that made me more tolerant of the species.

But a real turnabout in my equation with the Arachnoids occurred only after I made friends with a spider. I had surreptitiously stayed up, with a camouflaged light beyond my curfew hour of ten PM to finish reading the latest adventure of five find-outers and a dog, when I saw him. He was a large spender with hairy legs & a philosophical look. My fear of incurring parental wrath parental with for ignoring curfew norms kept me from bringing in the artillery. With a quick prayer I tucked my head under the pillow & was soon under the protection of Morpheus, albeit with nightmares of giant spiders. The next morning, he was still on the wall, but disappeared into a crevasse before. Mary started her spider patrol. I saw him next when I was in the midst of my bath & averse to doing a Archimedes encore, I steeled my resolve & tolerated his unabashed violation of my privacy. I soon got used to him. He would appear & gaze at me when I was reading or while I changed for school. He was never menacingly close & made no sudden moves- two tricks which he probably picked up from some animal handler in his prior life. He soon became an accepted occupant of my room.

One day a rather nasty looking hornet flew into my room. Buzzing around me, he eluded my attempts to ground him with my social studies text book & later with my badminton racquets. He would settle in strategic locations, like the back of a decorative light shade- where the danger of collateral damage would prevent me from launching an attack. The moment I sat down to read – he would start buzzing again. Spidey had been watching this tableau with an amused countenance. When I had knoched down the flower vase the fourth time he decided to intervene. The hornets foot got entangled in a bit of web near the night light & spidery sprang. Soon both creatures were locked in mortal combat, a clash of the titans – with each trying to get the other with his sting. The hornets' straggles were weakening & the web was tightening suddenly the web gave way under the combined weight of the combatants landing them both on the floor. Shaken by the fall Spidey's pincer grip relaxed & the hornet bugged off – out of the window in search of a safer nesting place. Spidey made his way back up the wall to his corner & I saluted him. It was nice to have friends, even amongst the denizen of hell.

****

THE MASQUERADE

Chatrapati Shivaji Railway terminus – erstwhile Victava Terminus (VT in popular parlance) is one the monuments of Mumbai. By a deft change of name, a government in power had garnered a million hearts & votes without a bead of sweet on there brows or an additional coat of whitewash on the British built monument. Fools toil to build monuments – the smart rechristen them to gainer credit.

I was on my way to Vishakhapatanam by the Konark express. after the last minute hiccups which characteristic most Indian rail journeys, I had settled at a window seat when there was a tap on the glass window. 'Dr. Mathai!' the young man at the window addressed me by the name [it did not strike me then, that he could have read it off the reservation]. Can you take a letter to my father, Dr. Hemantha Kumar at Vizag. I have

been trying to speak to him since morning – but the telephone lines are down. The man, about my age was well dressed and he passed me his visiting card which read Ananda Kumar, Proprietor Sai Traders.

Without waiting for my acquiescence, he hastily scribbled a note. The telephone numbers are there, he pointed to the top of the note – you give him a ring from Vizag Station & he will send his car to pick you up. I was flattered to have been recognised and pleased at the potential acquaintance with a professional senior colleague. As the letter was open, I could not help but glance at the contents.

The note read,

Tel:221401
Dear Papa,
We had an accident on the way back from
Sirdi – Mummy and Sarita are in the hospital,
but out of danger, please come down
immediately.
Anand

To
Dr. Hemantha Kumar, MD
Doctors' Plaza,
Vizag - 14

It would have been inhuman and
unprofessional not to query details. What
happened – I ventured to asked. Mr. Anand
appeared a bit reluctant to discuss details –
but I was doing his a favour he accused to

answer. "You must had read in the papers [I had not – but my interest in the Newspaper was usually confined to the sports page]". Our tourist bus over turned in the Ghats – 3 people died in the accident. We lost all our bags but fortunately non of us were seriously injured. I got away with this – he lifted up a trouser leg to reveal an Iodine soaked bandage – the type they apply for all wounds from cuts, scratches and blast injuries in a busy casualty. "My mother and sister are still in the hospital but are being discharged today".

The information provided was not compelling. If they are being discharged – why do not you go back to Vizag, I hated the thought of Mr. Hemantha Kumar losing out a busy practice for no reason. Mr. Anand seemed a trifle embarrassed. We lost our tickets and money in the accident. The Railways have offered to reissue the tickets at half rate – but we still need around Rs 500/-.

I handed over him Rs. 500/- which he accepted with a certain offended dignity. "I will phone up your father", I told him and will inform that you will be on tomorrows train. We will get in touch at Vizag, you must come over after we settle down again – I gave him my address and phone numbers and if he had asked for it would have probably given him by bank account number. After a gentlemanly clasp of hands, he left.

At Vishakhapatnam I attempted to contact a grateful Dr. Hemantha, informed by a recorded message that the number I had dialled did not exist. The next day the post man expressed the opinion that no Doctor's Plaza existed at Vizag-40. There were no phone calls from Mr. Anand. It took a couple of weeks for reality to sink in. I had been fleeced. Remonstrating myself to be more prudent in the future, I received that material losses did not matter much. Six months went by. A young colleague comes to me one day – Sir – do you know a Mr. Anand Kumar. He showed me a card – Mr. Anand Kumar, Proprietor – Sai Traders. Recognition flashed- Go On – I urged my friend- what happened.

Well sir! I met him in the train two weeks ago. He had been pick-pocketed. He told me that you were a close friend, how you would visit him every Sunday for a traditional Andhra meal. He had your telephone numbers & address. I lent him Rs. 500. – but have not been able to trace him thereafter. Mr. Anand Kumar is possibly out there even today – unless he has moved on to higher ranks of deception, like politics or as Government certified contractor.

****

THE RUNNER

The runner longed to the Athletic Association of Ajmer – a prestigious and respected organisation which fostered and nurtured the collective aspiration of its members towards an organised excellence [quoting from the Ajmer Athletic Association (AAA) information palm-plate]. The runner believed in the association's motto – Aspire to excel. He would get up every morning at 4:30 to scorch the road and awaken the stray dogs with his running – his was a punishing, self-designed workout – pushing himself to the extreme chalking award 100 kms, stoically luxuriating in the pain and bruises.

The AAA's president was a dynamic charismatic administrator who had the National sports organisation literally eating out of his hand. It was roumered that he had ear of the secretary of the international Olympic association. Under his leadership the AAA had diversified. early in his tenure, the president had with the vision born of genius come to the seemingly startling conclusion that the future of the AAA was not in sport. 'There will always be fools burning themselves. We have look beyond these sweaty fools if we are to achieve anything'- he confided to his Lieutenants. So the AAA diversified. The infrastructure, the vast playing grounds & the stadium created by a colonial power at their prime was optimally exploited. The Ajmer Athletic Association, the president emphasised was not solely about sport. It was about social issues, national development, world peace & preserving the habitat of the engendered possum. Pictures of the president holding a baby possum graced the front page of national newspapers. The chief ministers' daughter's wedding was just one of the magnificent functions held at the AAA stadium.

The president was indeed a visionary. Diversification & some deft net watching saw Ajmer explode as a centre for sport development. A three kilometer walk for health organised by the association aroused international interest. Photographs of the association president, with the minister on his left and Julia Roberts on his right, walking the talk made it to international tabloids- the mega event was sponsored by the international shoe giant Medibox. Ten thousand Medibox shoes were bought by the association from the National Sports Funds [created by an act of Parliament for upliftment of under privileged sportspersons from backward communities], and distributed amongst the delegates. Many honours were bestowed by the

President on various dignitaries on behalf of the AAA including the 'emeritus professorship of sports excellence' to the minister of the state for sport. The munificence of the president was reciprocated and his achievement would remain the stuff of legend for years at come.

It was at an informal meeting with the subjects that the runner committed a major gaffe. He asked – 'but what about athletics

– when we completed the 42 km marathon, there was no one to offer us a glass of water.

The President frowned & turned away. His coterie and aspiring coterie surrounded him with apologues & supplications. Surely the runner had no place in this organisation of excellence with such an enigmatic leader at the helm.

Please tell us again – a pot-bellied office bearer of the AAA urged the president – about the time you, won the needle and thread race. Your achievements are such an inspiration to us, the younger lot. The President smiled –content.

****

THE ATHEIST

The youth was a rebel in every sense of the word. He rebelled against authority, as a kid he rebelled when he was asked to drink milk, as he grew up he rebelled against home work – against the school uniform & against his mother when she refused him permission to stay back after school for football. May be it was the diet of fresh fish curry & rice, against a back drop of communism & student unrest or the relative isolation of growing up bereft of the sobering influence of friends or siblings.

There was a veritable library at home, for father had been an arm chair philosopher whose tastes in literature ranged from Dante to Gordan & PG wood house. The effect of uncensored literature or a developing mind contributed to his non conformism.

A natural extension of rebellion against human authority is the questioning of the heavenly one – and by the time the youth was in college, he was a professed atheist.

Religion – the opium of the masses was invented by smart men to control the proletariat, he averred. God was a figment of one's imagination, a creature of convenience and the vicarious enforcer of a code of conduct which suited big brother.

The youth would sprout Darwinian hypothesis on the evolution of the species. He had his own pet theory on the origin of the universe. If a negative and a positive could nullify each other result in a Zero – surely a universe and an anti-universe could be evolved from nothingness. No argument could sway the youths' convictions and the elders would turn away muttering – "arrogant fool".

As time is the best healer – it is also a great modulator of excesses. With passing years, the youth was tempered by influences both good and bad to the realization and acceptance of powers and concerns beyond his own. His active atheism merged into an agnosticism which later evolved into acceptance and dependence in the power, presence and compassion of the almighty.

He tended to pray more and soon realized that Divine intervention often occurred before he appreciated the gravity or significance of issues, threats were thwarted before he was aware of their existence and that the most dire of dangers were the once he was unaware of.

The youth's conviction of the lack of God and in his own infallibility were both eroded by the passage of time. Failures and frustration forged euphoric youth to the wisdom of the ages. Occasionally he would muse over his earlier pet theories on the evolution of the universe. There was a certain pride in the reminiscence on the originality of thought at a tender age. It was during one of those moments of unconscious self appreciation that he remembered the first few lines of the book of Genesis – "In the beginning there was nothing – and out of nothing is God created the heavens and the Earth" – The youth realized that he had not been so original after all.

****

THE DECADENCE OF THE DAMNED

Mr. Patwardhan was offended and when his ire was aroused, his Hitlerian moustache would quiver like the quills of an irked porcupine. 'It is people like you, he chided his sixteen years old niece Kumkum, Kumkum had being staying with them the weakened, to get away from the ragging at medical school. It is people like you, he continued, who perpetuate the cycle of poverty in our great nation. You encourage dependence and with it, poverty by dishing out alms. One should have a sense of social responsibility'- The barrage continued unabated. The oratorical skills of Patwardhan within the confines of a captive audience were unparalleled. Without dvelving further into the affair or the nitty gritties of the Patwardhan disposition let us

- like a lawyer would say, examine the facts of the case.

The Patwardhan couple had taken their visiting niece for a movie at the Inox theatre complex. Mr Patwardhan was returning from the basement, where he had parked his antique Fiat (antique by age, not value). He witnessed, with horror and with consternation, his niece parting with a ten rupee note to a beggar women toting an infant on her shoulder & impudence in her demeanour.

Mr. Patwardhan could be described as socially aware & active individual. He was a member of the Grameena Suraksha Association, treasurer of small scale beedimaker brotherhood & contributed Rs. 50 every year to save the tiger fund. He was never at a loss for words when topics like the effect of the influence of multinational companies on traditional Indian moral values come up for discussion.

There was undeniable merit in the Patwardhan view point – KumKum sensed. Easy money perpetuates a desire for easier pickings. Charity was possibly the oldest instrument after matrimony for subjugation of the free spirit. KumKum was suitably chastised. With the prudence of castigated youth, sulked despite Mrs Patwardhan attempts at mollification. "Lagae Rahoe Munna Bhai" soothed the sting of Uncle Patty's caustic remarks & an ice cream at the Baskin Robins cooled emotions all around. Patty uncle was not really a bad sort of fellow – KumKum rationalized & there was definite merit in his argument.

The next morning, as was the custom, KumKum – with a tote bag of goodies to last her the weak & a lab coat slung over her right arm-(as she planned to go straight to her lecture hall) waited at the Pool Gate bus stop. She studiously ignored the street urchin tugging at her sleeve with one dirty paw while the other stubbed his tummy in a dramatization of calorie deprivation. The Patwardhan dictum – it seems, had sunk in. The five rupees coin she left in her purse slumbered undisturbed.

KumKum glanced at her digital watch – it was 07:55, in another five minutes the bus which would whisk her to the Dondipedah junction for the princely fare of six rupees & seventy five paise would arrive. She would reach Dondipedah at 08:10. A brisk walk of a hundred yards would see her at the college portal & at 08:15 she would be ensconced in her seat in the anatomy lecture hall. It was fatal to be late for Prof. Ganga Walkers lecture. Ganga walk was singular in self opinioned wit. His caustic commands on the antecedents of the late comers were a subject of wholesome mirth to all except his victim of the day.

KumKum glanced at her watch again 07:55 - what the –A bead of perspiration broke out on her brow. She glanced at the oversized imitation Rolex of a college Romeo who had been for the past quarter appreciating her from various vantage angles. It was 08:10. I am dead, KumKum muttered to herself - her watch had betrayed her – she had missed the bus. Oh God –Oh God – she muttered herself – please help.

A pale blue Santro with dents on both bumpers suggesting ownership by a member of the fairer sex stopped. A lady peeked out- "KumKum- you want a lift?" it was

Mrs. Mary, taught at the dental wing of the college and was a friend of the Patwardhan family. With a grateful heart, Kumkum hopped into to the car. As Mrs. Mary engaged gears with a creak and growl that would make any

Santro mechanic wince – KumKum tapped her arm – 'auntie- one second please'.

The street urchin had followed her to the Santro & stood with his nose flattened against the glass. A ten-rupee note changed hands & the car moved on.

Charity, KumKum surmised (we call it luck – when it comes from God) – needs to be shared.

****